WACKY
WEDNESDAY

By
Dr. Seuss

WACKY
WEDNESDAY

By
Dr. Seuss

writing as
Theo. LeSieg

Illustrated by George Booth

HarperCollins *Children's Books*

™ & © Dr. Seuss Enterprises, L.P.
All Rights Reserved

A CIP catalogue record for this title is available from the
British Library.
No part of this publication may be reproduced, stored
in a retrieval system or transmitted in any form or by
any means, electronic, mechanical, photocopying,
recording or otherwise, without the prior permission of
HarperCollins Publishers Ltd, 1 London Bridge Street
London SE1 9GF

1 3 5 7 9 10 8 6 4 2

ISBN 978-0-00-823996-1

© 1974 by Dr. Seuss Enterprises, L.P.
All Rights Reserved
Illustrations © 1974 by Random House Inc.
Published by arrangement with Random House Inc.,
New York, USA
First published in the UK 1975
This edition published in the UK 2017 by
HarperCollins *Children's Books,*
a division of HarperCollins*Publishers* Ltd
1 London Bridge Street
London SE1 9GF

www.harpercollins.co.uk

Printed in China

PART OF A SET. NOT FOR INDIVIDUAL RESALE

It all began
with that shoe on the wall.
A shoe on a wall . . . ?
Shouldn't be there at all!

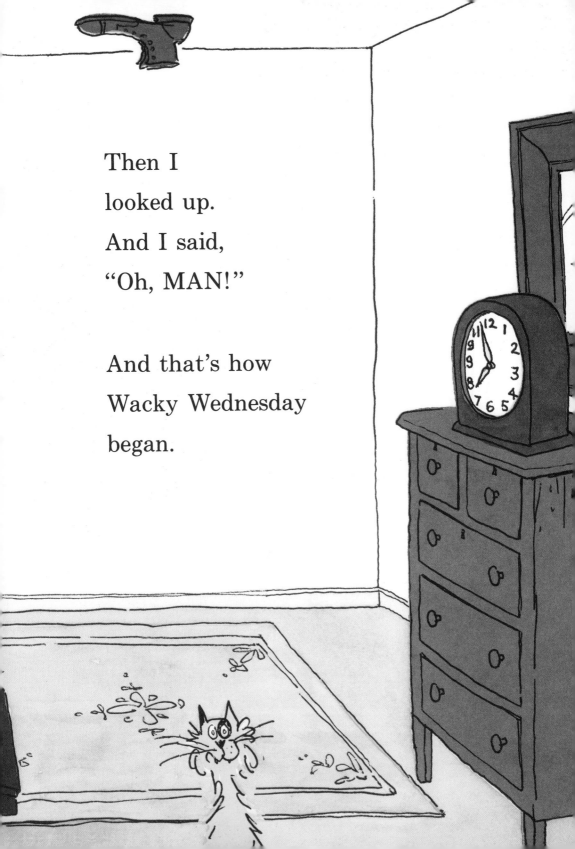

Then I
looked up.
And I said,
"Oh, MAN!"

And that's how
Wacky Wednesday
began.

I looked out
the window.
And I said,
"GEE!"

More things were wacky!
And I saw three.

I went
down the hall
and I said,
"HEY!"

Three
more things
were wacky today!

In the
bathroom,
MORE!

In the
bathroom,
FOUR!

I began to dress.
Then I said,
"WOW!"

Four MORE things
were wacky now!

I looked
in the kitchen.
I said,
"By cracky!
Five more things
are very wacky!"

I was late for school.

I started along.

And I saw that

six more things were wrong.

And then seven more!

And the Sutherland sisters!
They looked wacky, too.

They said,
"Nothing is wacky
around here but you!"

"But look!" I yelled.
"Eight things are wrong
here at school."

"Nothing is wrong,"
they said.
"Don't be a fool."

I ran into school.

I yelled to Miss Bass . . .

. . . "Look!
Nine things
are wacky
right here
in your class!"

"Nothing is wacky
here in my class!
Get out!
You're the wacky one!
OUT!"
said Miss Bass.

I went out
the school door.
Things were worse than before.
I couldn't believe it.
Ten wacky things more!

FOUR SALE

Then I
counted
ELEVEN!

Then . . .
twelve WORSE things!
I got scared.
And I ran.

I ran
and knocked over
Patrolman McGann.

"I'm sorry, Patrolman."

That's all I could say.

"Don't be sorry," he smiled.
"It's that kind of a day.
But be glad!
Wacky Wednesday
will soon go away!"

"Only twenty things more
will be wacky," he said.

"Just find them
and then
you can go
back to bed."

Wacky Wednesday was gone

when I counted them all.

And I even got rid

of that shoe on the wall.